Quentin Blake's
NURSERY RHYME BOOK

RED FOX

CPi
QUANTUM

PRINTED ON ARROW SILK 140GSM

QUENTIN BLAKE'S NURSERY RHYME BOOK
A RED FOX BOOK 978 1 849 41690 0

First published in Great Britain by Jonathan Cape,
an imprint of Random House Children's Books
A Random House Group Company

Jonathan Cape edition published 1983
Red Fox edition first published 1995
This Red Fox edition published 2012

The author and publishers are grateful to Oxford University Press for permission
to use the rhymes, some from Iona and Peter Opie's *Oxford Dictionary of
Nursery Rhymes* (1951) and some from their *Oxford Nursery Rhyme Book* (1955).

1 3 5 7 9 10 8 6 4 2

Copyright © Quentin Blake, 1983

Red Fox Books are published by Random House Children's Books,
61–63 Uxbridge Road, London W5 5SA

www.**kids**at**randomhouse**.co.uk
www.**randomhouse**.co.uk

Addresses for companies within The Random House Group Limited can be found at:
www.randomhouse.co.uk/offices.htm

THE RANDOM HOUSE GROUP Limited Reg. No. 954009

A CIP catalogue record for this book is available from the British Library.

The Random House Group Limited supports the Forest Stewardship Council (FSC®),
the leading international forest certification organization. Our books carrying the FSC
label are printed on FSC®-certified paper. FSC is the only forest certification scheme
endorsed by the leading environmental organizations, including Greenpeace. Our paper
procurement policy can be found at www.randomhouse.co.uk/environment.

Little Jack Sprat
　　Once had a pig,
It was not very little,
　　Nor yet very big,
It was not very lean,
　　It was not very fat –
It's a good pig to grunt,
　　Said little Jack Sprat.

Ickle ockle, blue bockle,
Fishes in the sea,

If you want a pretty maid,
Please choose me.

Jeremiah,
    blow the fire,
        Puff, puff, puff.

First you blow it gently

Then you blow it rough.

Handy spandy, Jack-a-Dandy
Loves plum cake and sugar candy.
He bought some at a
grocer's shop

And out he came,
hop, hop,
hop, hop!

Gregory Griggs,
Gregory Griggs,
Had twenty-seven
different wigs.

He wore them up,
he wore them down
To please the people
of the town;

He wore them east,
   he wore them west,
But he never could tell
   which he loved the best.

Dickery, dickery, dare,
  The pig flew up in the air;

The man in brown
    soon brought him down,
Dickery, dickery, dare.

I had a little husband
    No bigger than my thumb;
I put him in a pint pot
    And there I bid him drum.
I gave him some garters
    To garter up his hose,
And a little silk handkerchief
    To wipe his pretty nose.

Pussy Cat ate the dumplings,
　　Pussy Cat ate the dumplings,
Mama stood by,
　　And cried, Oh, fie!
　　Why did you eat
　　　　the dumplings?

William McTrimbletoe,
He's a good fisherman,

Catches fishes

Puts them in dishes,

Catches hens
Puts them in pens,

Some lay eggs

Some lay none

William McTrimbletoe,
He doesn't eat one.

Pretty John Watts,
We are troubled with rats,
Will you drive them out of the house?

We have mice, too, in plenty
That feast in the pantry,
But let them stay,
And nibble away:
What harm is a little brown mouse?

Little Blue Ben,
       who lives in the glen,
Keeps a blue cat
       and one blue hen

Which lays of blue eggs
        a score and ten;
Where shall I find
        the little Blue Ben?

Goosey, goosey gander,
    Who stands yonder?
        Little Betsy Baker;

Take her up
and shake her.

Terence McDiddler,

The three-stringed fiddler,

Can charm, if you please,

The fish from the seas!

Robin the Bobbin
the big-bellied Ben
He ate more meat
than fourscore men.

He ate a cow
he ate a calf
He ate a butcher
and a half

He ate a church
    he ate a steeple
He ate a priest
    and all the people

A cow and a calf
A butcher and a half
A church and a steeple
And all the good people

And yet he complained
    That his stomach wasn't
        full.

Here I am
Little Jumping Joan;

When nobody's with me
I'm all alone.

Oh, Mother,
I shall be married
   To Mr Punchinello,

To Mr Punch,
   To Mr Joe,
      To Mr Nell,
         To Mr Lo,

Mr Punch, Mr Joe,
Mr Nell, Mr Lo,
　　To Mr Punchinello!

Some other books by
Quentin Blake

All Join In
Angel Pavement
Angelica Sprocket's Pockets
Angelo
Clown
Cockatoos
Fantastic Daisy Artichoke
The Green Ship
Jack and Nancy
Loveykins
Mister Magnolia
Mrs Armitage and the Big Wave
Mrs Armitage on Wheels
Mrs Armitage Queen of the Road
Patrick
Quentin Blake's ABC
A Sailing Boat in the Sky
Snuff
Zagazoo